This Orchard
book belongs to

....

....

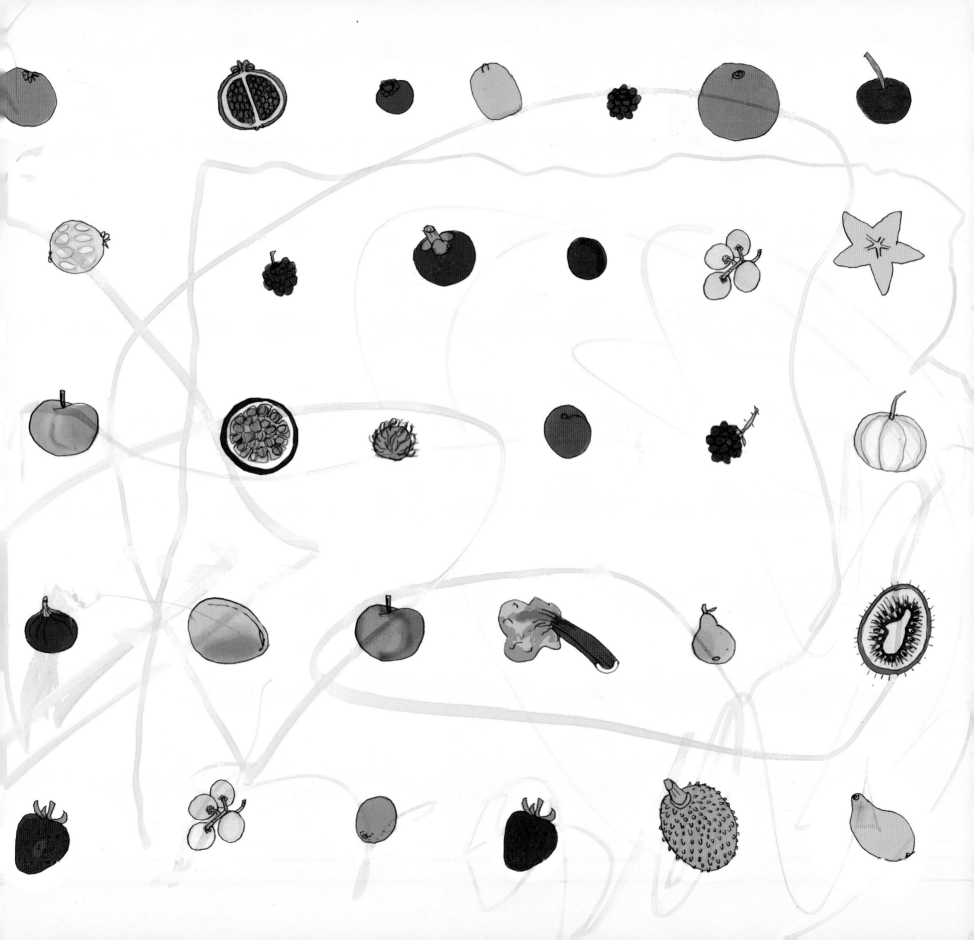

For Imogen Brooke - M.R.

To my girls, Lizzie and Alice - L.T.

First published in 2012 by Orchard Books
First published in paperback in 2013

ISBN 978 1 40830 855 4

Text © Michelle Robinson 2012
Illustrations © Lauren Tobia 2012

A CIP catalogue record for this book is available from the British Library.

1 3 5 7 9 10 8 6 4 2

Printed in China

Orchard Books is a division of Hachette Children's Books,
an Hachette UK company.
www.hachette.co.uk

How to Find

a Fruit Bat

Michelle Robinson Lauren Tobia

ORCHARD

If you're not too fond of fruit,
may I suggest you find yourself
a fruit bat?

They're furry, they're friendly –
and they'll eat ALL
your fruit for you.
Imagine never having to
eat a piece of fruit again.

Not even a single grape!

It's the perfect plan. So, what are you waiting for?

Let's find a fruit bat!

First things first:

fruit bats don't live in your neighbourhood. You'll have to go to a whole other country to find one.

Start by building a boat.

This may seem extreme, but just think of all the raspberries you'll have to eat if you don't.

Excellent!

Now pack a bag
full of fruit – for
the fruit bat.

And set sail.

It's a long journey,

but at this rate we'll be
back in time for
a fruit-free supper.

That's the easy
bit out of the way.
Time for a little trek
through the jungle . . .

Surely you'd rather walk through
a tigery jungle than spend the
rest of your life eating rhubarb?

That's the spirit!

Now just cross the little stream and climb the tiny hill . . .

. . . then step into the deep, dark cave.
Don't worry about what might be

lurking inside!

Think happy thoughts instead, like never
having to eat another pineapple ring.

Get a move on;
it's nearly
supper time!

Oops!
Try again.

Perfect.

This is just the sort of place
where fruit bats live.
Look around for something
small and **furry**.

And again.

And again.

Congratulations!
You've found a
fruit bat!

I told you
they were
friendly.

Let's head
home and have
some supper . . .

What do you mean,
you don't know
the way back?

It's dark!

It's creepy!

It's supper time!

And there's nothing to eat . . .

except . . .

FRUIT!

Hmm . . . perhaps **peaches** are perfect at **picnics.**

And who would
have thought
tangerines
were so popular?

Bananas
are rather tasty
when **toasted!**

And, hold on . . .

. . . raspberries
don't taste so bad when
you're hanging around
with friends.

It's time to sail home for supper!

That's enough jungles,

enough trekking

and enough fruit
for one day, too.

Oh, go on then.
Maybe just **one**
more grape!

Mmm...Yummy!

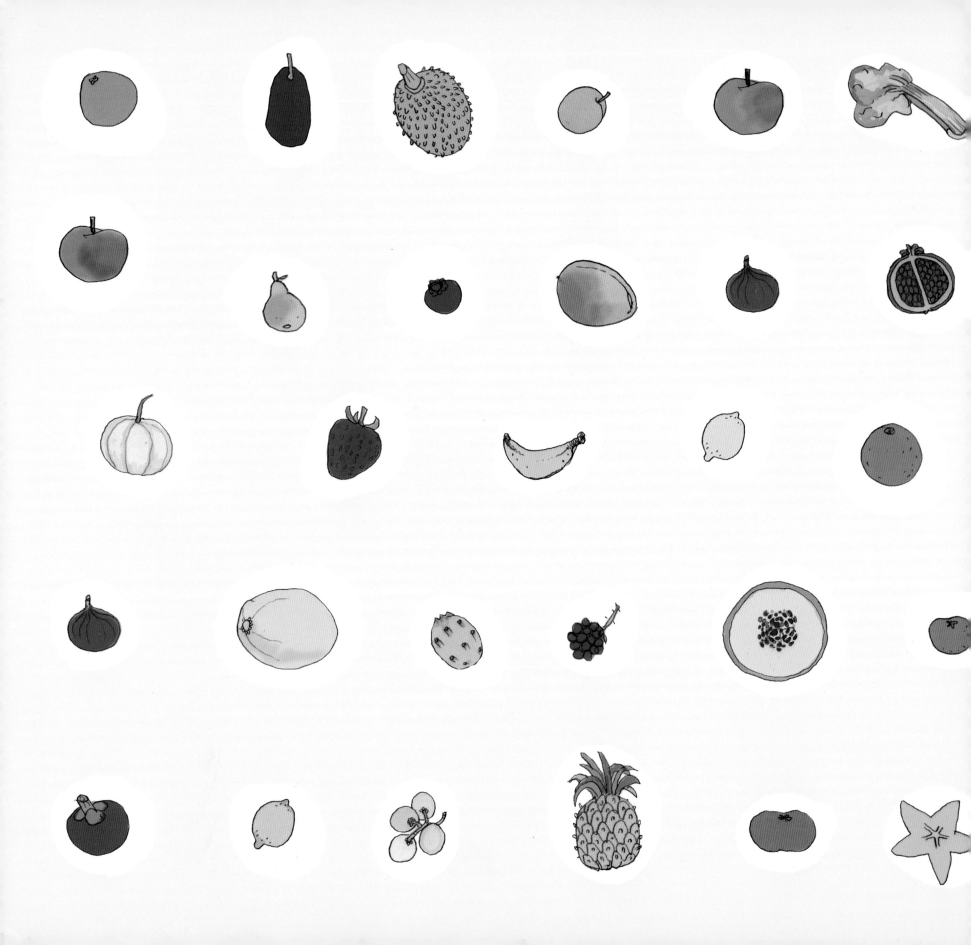

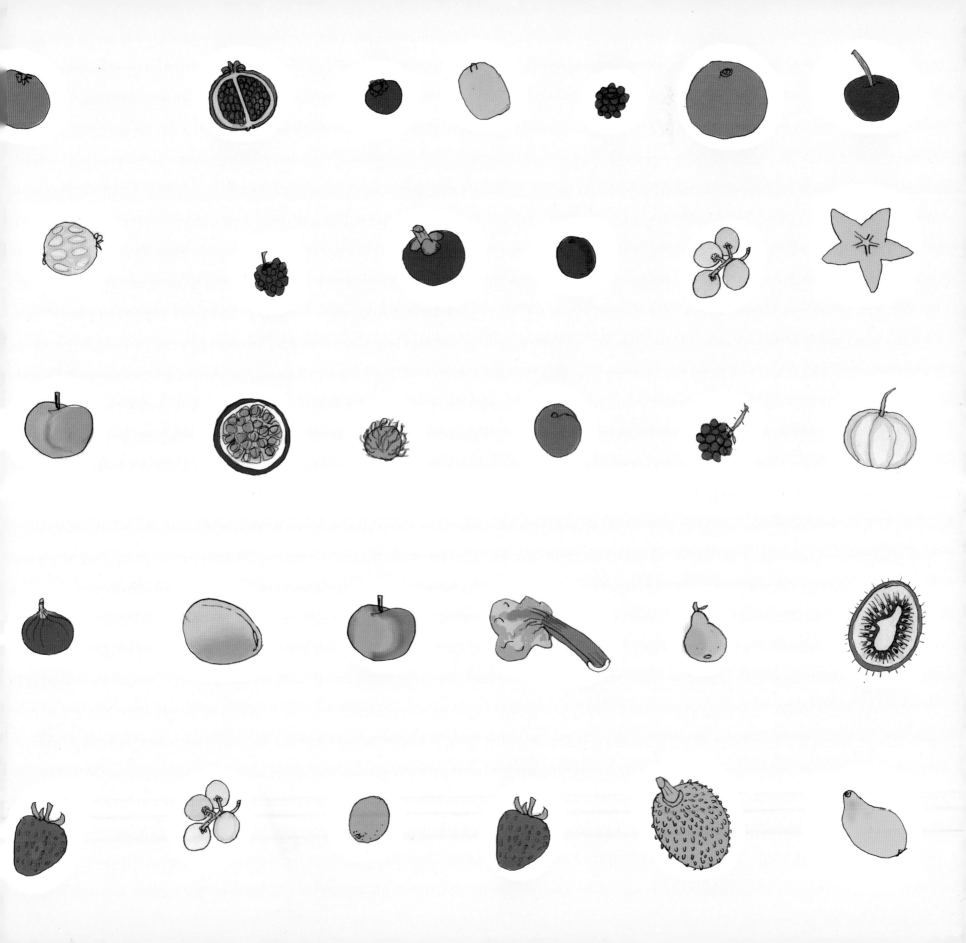

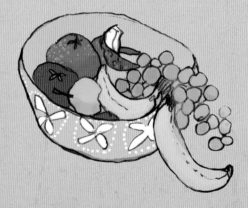